For my beautiful boys—Scott, Jordan, and Jonathan. —K.C.

To Papa—why is your granddaughter so beautiful?
Because my Papa was so handsome. —Z.P.

A FEIWEL AND FRIENDS BOOK

An imprint of Macmillan Publishing Group, LLC

120 Broadway, New York, NY 10271

YOU BE MOMMY. Text copyright © 2020 by Karla Clark.
Illustrations copyright © 2020 by Zoe Persico. All rights reserved.
Printed in China by RR Donnelley Asia Printing Solutions Ltd.,
Dongguan City, Guangdong Province.

Our books may be purchased in bulk for promotional,
educational, or business use. Please contact your local bookseller
or the Macmillan Corporate and Premium Sales
Department at (800) 221-7945 ext. 5442 or by email
at MacmillanSpecialMarkets@macmillan.com.

Library of Congress Control Number: 2019940855
ISBN 978-1-250-22538-2

Book design by Carol Ly

Feiwel and Friends logo designed by Filomena Tuosto

First edition, 2020

10 9 8 7 6 5 4 3 2 1

mackids.com

You Be Mommy

written by
KARLA CLARK

FEIWEL AND FRIENDS
NEW YORK

illustrated by
ZOE PERSICO

Mommy's too tired to be Mommy tonight.
Can you be Mommy and hold me tight?

Read me a story and pat my tummy?
Wipe my nose when it gets runny?

Check for monsters under the bed?
Sing me a song and rub my head?

Can you be Mommy and kiss me good night?
Mommy's too tired to be Mommy tonight.

She worked all day at the computer store.

Came home to a big mess on the floor!

Helped with homework—even MATH!

Fed the dog and gave him a bath.

Drove Sarah to soccer and Tommy to chess.
Sewed a button on your favorite dress.

Cleaned the laundry and ironed the shirts.
Patched up the boo-boos and hurty-hurts.

Can you be Mommy and turn off the light?

Mommy's too tired to be Mommy tonight.

She cooked the dinner and did the dishes.
Tried her best to grant all your wishes.
Made ice cream sundaes with extra-large scoops.

And now her eyes will not stay open.

That you'll be Mommy and tuck me in.

That you'll be the one to kiss my chin.

So lend me your blankie and rock me to sleep.

And as I drift, help me count sheep.

Mommy's just too tired to stay awake.
Oh, please be Mommy, for goodness' sake!

What's that you say? You're tired, too?
You'd rather ME be Mommy instead of you?

Oh, all right then, I'll let you win.
One more big yawn . . .

and I'll be Mommy again.

For you'll always be my little treasure.
And I'll be Mommy forever and ever.